Read with me
The day trip

by WILLIAM MURRAY
stories by JILL CORBY
illustrated by JON DAVIS

"Come on, please," says the teacher. "Come over here and get on now. Up you go. We can all get on now.

''Tom, you sit here with John. Kate, you can sit over there with Suki.

''I can put your lunch boxes up here. Now we must all sit down and we can go.''

"Look, Suki," says Kate, "there is my home. And there is my mum."

"My home is over there," says Suki. "My mum is not there. She is at work. She likes to work."

"My home is down there," says John. "I can't see my mum at all."

"Look at the boats on the water. We can go faster," says Tom.

"Here are your things. Now you can get out," the teacher tells them.

"Wait here for everyone to get out," she says.

"They are all out now. Everyone is here," says Suki. "We can go up there."

"We must get over here," says
Kate. "I can have your things,
and you jump down."

"We must go up here with
them," Suki tells her.

"Look at all these dragonflies," says Kate. "They are all round here. There are lots of dragonflies here, and there are more over by the water," she tells Suki.

They look at the dragonflies.
They see lots more of them by
the trees. Kate tells the teacher
that she likes dragonflies.
''Just look at all these,'' she
says.

"I can't get over there," says John. "Please help me to get over, Tom."

"Give me your lunch box," says Tom, "and then I can help you."

"Please help me," says Suki to Tom.

"Give me your lunch box, and then I can help you over," Tom tells her.

Tom helps them all.
"There, now we are all over," he
says.

Now they are down by the
water.
"Where can we get over?" asks
Kate.

"Look at all the rabbits," says
Suki. "I want to play with
them."

The teacher tells them that they have to go down by the tree, then they can get over the water.
"Now you can play with the rabbits," Tom tells Suki and Kate.

"Where have the rabbits gone?" asks Kate.

"They have all gone," says Suki.

They play by the water.
''I like it here,'' says Tom.

''There are lots of fish down
here,'' says John, ''and some
more over there.''

Then they see some big fish.
"That is a big one," says Tom,
"I must get one of these.

"I can get that big one there,"
Tom tells John.

"No, you can't. It's gone now,"
John says.

"Where has Tom got to?" the teacher asks.

"He is down there by the water," John tells her.

"Just look at me," says Tom. "Please help me. I can't get out."

"I can help him to get out,"
John tells the teacher.

"I have got to help you to get
out," says John. And he helps
him out of the water.

"The fish have
all gone now,"
says Kate.

"You must not go in there, Kate," says Suki. "It says, DANGER. KEEP OUT."

Kate reads, "DANGER. KEEP OUT.

"We can't go in there," she tells John. "It says, DANGER. KEEP OUT.

"It's to keep us out," she says.

"Where has the teacher gone?"
asks Kate.

"We can't see her and she can't
see us," Suki says.

"I know where we must go,"
Tom tells them. "Just up here."

"We can eat our lunch here," says John.

"Yes, we can sit here to eat our lunch," Tom says.

"Where is your lunch box?" Kate asks Tom.

"I don't know," says Tom. "I don't know where it is."

"I can give you some of this to
eat," says John.

"And you can have one of
these," Kate tells him.

"We like to sit here and eat our
lunch," John says.

They want to play in the trees.
"You hide first," Kate tells them.
"I can stay here. You can all go
and hide in there," she says.

"She can't see us here," says
Tom.

Kate looks for them. She sees
John first, and then Suki and
Tom.

"Now I can hide," she tells Tom,
"and you can look for all of us."
They hide in the trees.

They play here now. They like to jump down. There is no danger here.

''You have your go first,'' says John. ''And then it's my turn.''

"You have had your turn," Kate
tells him. "It's Tom's turn. It's
his turn now.

"Now Tom's had his go and it's
my turn. This is fun," she says.

"I can see my mother," says Kate. "My mum is there to help. Is your mum there?"

"No," says Suki. "My mum is at work in our shop."

"Shall we go over there?" asks Kate. "Shall we go and see?"

"Yes, we must go over there to see them. Look, they can see us," Suki says.

"It's a hot day. I shall take this off," says Tom.

"Yes, it is a hot day. I shall take this off," says Suki.

"Don't put them there," Tom's mum tells him. "Give them to me."
He gives her his things.

"Can we go up there now?"
Kate asks her mother.

"You must ask your teacher
first," her mother tells her.

The teacher says, "Yes, off you
go."

"Now we are up here,"
says Kate.

"Look, we can see our school over there," Suki tells her. "It's a hot day down there, and it's hot up here."

They sit down.

"Shall we take more things off?" asks Kate.

"I know," says Suki. "We can take these off."

"Take them off and put them here," says Kate.

They are not so hot now.

They go down. Round and round, over and over, down and down, faster and faster.

"Just look at us," they say.

"Come and eat now," the teacher tells them. "You can have the first one, John. Here is a big one for you, Suki, and a big one for you, Kate.

"I have some more here," says the teacher. "Has everyone had some?"

John and Tom want some more.

"Everyone, get all your things, please," says the teacher, "so that we can go.

"Don't go up there now, please. I want you to get all your things. Tom, have you got your lunch box? Where can it have gone?" his teacher asks him.

"I don't know where it is," he says.

"Kate and Suki, you can't go like that. Where have your things gone? You must go and look for them," the teacher says.

"Mum, where has Sam got to?" asks Kate.

"He was over there," her mother says. "He was there, by the trees.

"I don't know where he is now," she says.

"There you are, Sam," says Tom. "Just look at him. He has got my lunch box."

"You can't eat now, Tom," the teacher tells him. "You have had a lot to eat. Come on, we must go."

"Your mum was at work.
Is she here now?" Kate asks Suki.

"Yes, look," says Suki. "Here
she comes now. She has come
to take me home."

The mothers take them all home.
Tom and Kate go home with
Mother and Sam.

It was so hot that day and they
had lots of fun.

Words introduced in this book

Number of words.......................43

What has Sam got?
Where did he find it?
Do you have a lunch box?

LADYBIRD READING SCHEMES

Ladybird reading schemes are suitable for use with any other method of learning to read.

Say the Sounds

Ladybird's **Say the Sounds** graded reading scheme is a *phonics* scheme. It teaches children the sounds of individual letters and letter combinations, enabling them to tackle new words by building them up as a blend of smaller units.

There are 8 titles in this scheme:

1 **Rocket to the jungle**
2 **Frog and the lollipops**
3 **The go-cart race**
4 **Pirate's treasure**
5 **Humpty Dumpty and the robots**
6 **Flying saucer**
7 **Dinosaur rescue**
8 **The accident**

Support material available: Practice Books, Double Cassette Pack, Flash Cards